Levi and the Little Loaf

Menucha Fuchs

Levi and the Little Loaf
by Menucha Fuchs

Publisher:
Kav L'kav—Menucha Fuchs Books
P.O.B. 50198
Jerusalem, Israel
Phone/Fax: 972-2-581-5791

ISBN 1-932443-38-X

Translated by: Nachum Shapiro
Adapted by: Toby Cohen
Illustrations by: Ahuva Perlov
Layout by: Rahel Lowy

Distributed by:

The Judaica Press, Inc.
123 Ditmas Ave.
Brooklyn, NY 11218
800 972-6201 / 718-972-6200
Fax 718-972-6204
www.judaicapress.com

Printed in Israel

Every night, Levi's father would call: "Oh, Levi, it's time to take your bath."

Levi would start to complain: "I don't *want* to take a bath. Please don't make me! The water is too hot, and the shampoo gets in my eyes. Do I *have* to?"

But his father always made him take a bath.

One night, his father said, "Levi, if you take your bath without complaining, I will tell you a story."

"While I take my bath?" asked Levi.

"Oh, yes! Now, hop in." And his father began:

Once there was a bakery owned by a kind-hearted baker named Baruch. Every day, Baruch the Baker worked hard. He took flour and water, and mixed them in a large mixing bowl. Then he would add different things, like sugar, salt, yeast, some oil or eggs, and make delicious bread, rolls, pita and challah.

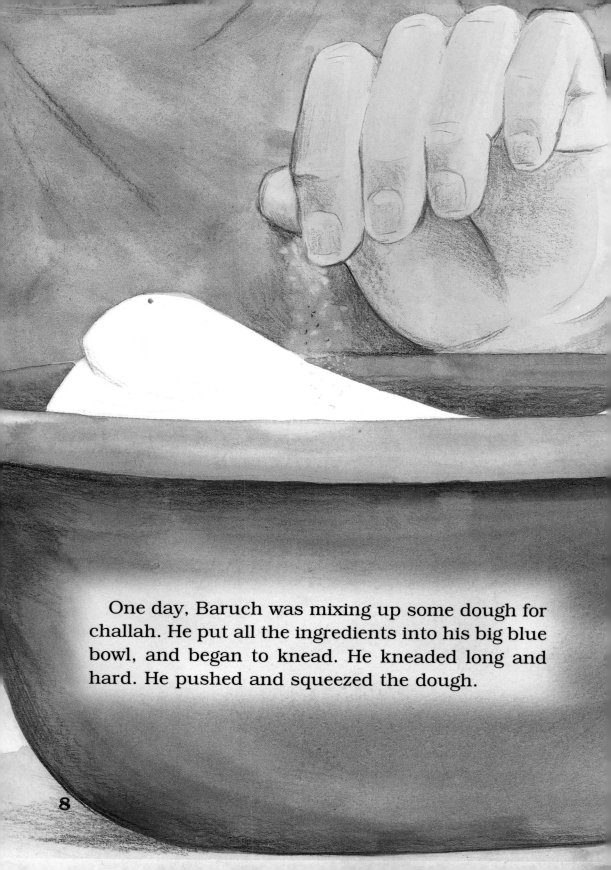

One day, Baruch was mixing up some dough for challah. He put all the ingredients into his big blue bowl, and began to knead. He kneaded long and hard. He pushed and squeezed the dough.

SUGAR

SALT

Suddenly, he heard a strange noise, like someone crying, "Ow, ow!"
He looked around, and saw no one.
"Who said that?" Baruch asked, confused.

"It is I, your dough," came a voice from the mound under his hand. "You are kneading me so roughly," complained the dough. "I don't like to be poked and smashed."

"I'm sorry," said Baruch kindly, "but I have no choice. I am a baker. If I want you to be tasty and bake properly, I have to knead you very well."

And he kneaded it some more. Then he began to punch and pound the dough, over and over.

"Ow, ow! Stop!" cried the dough.

"What is the matter now?" asked Baruch.
"You are hitting me too hard," the dough moaned. "You're hurting me!"

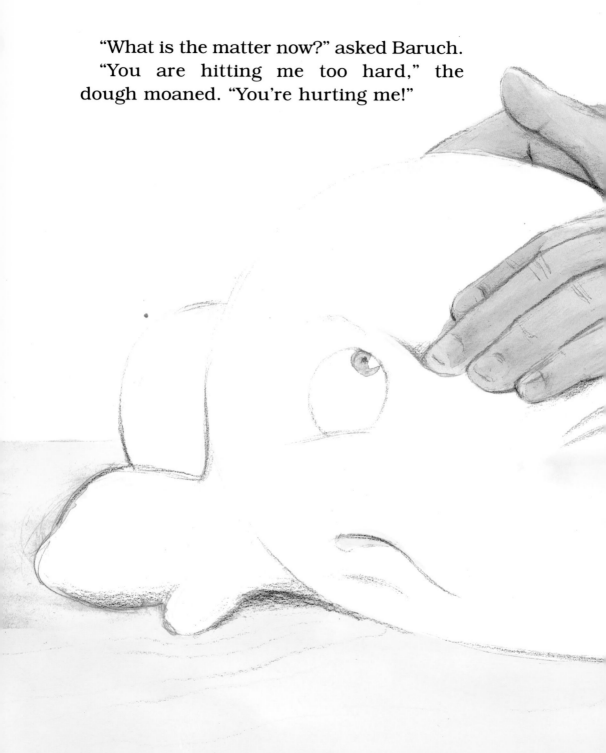

Baruch patted the dough. "There, now," he smiled.
"You want to be a good, strong dough, don't you?"

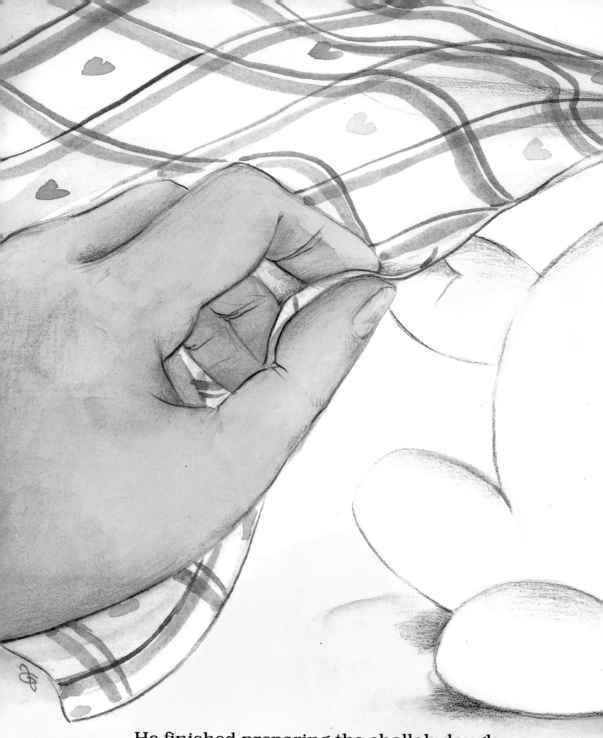

He finished preparing the challah dough,
and put a cotton cloth over it to keep it
warm. That would help it rise nicely.

But he heard a muffled, "Hey!"

"What is it now?" he sighed. He lifted the cloth.

"Don't cover me," complained the dough. "I don't like to be in the dark."

17

"Oh, dear." Baruch shook his head slowly.
"Little dough, you must learn to be patient,"
he said. "You want to rise, so you can become
a beautiful challah, don't you?"

So the dough sat and waited for a long time, and it grew, and grew and GREW.

Finally, it got tired of waiting.
"Hey!" it shouted.
"Yes?" asked Baruch.
"I'm tired of waiting," complained the dough.

"I am sorry. You will have to wait a little
more," explained Baruch. "A dough has to
rise to twice its size. We have no choice."

21

When the dough was ready, Baruch returned. He said a special *bracha*, and pinched off a piece of the dough.

"Ow!" shrieked the dough. "Why are you hurting me again?"

"This is a special *mitzvah* for a special dough. It is called separating challah. I have to pinch you to do the *mitzvah*."

23

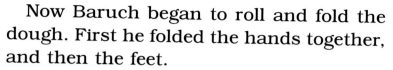

Now Baruch began to roll and fold the dough. First he folded the hands together, and then the feet.

"Hey, hey!" cried the dough. "I don't like to be folded up like this," he complained.

"Now, be patient, little dough," said Baruch. "You are going to be a beautifully shaped challah, but only if you are folded tightly."

Baruch finished the folding, and, lo and behold! The dough looked like a real challah!

Baruch carried it to the oven. He opened the heavy oven door, and the room filled with waves of heat.

"Ow, ow!" It was the dough again.

Baruch looked down. "Is there a problem?"

"I am afraid the heat will hurt me," complained the dough.

"I am sorry, but you need not be afraid. The hot oven is good for you. It turns you into delicious bread," explained Baruch.

27

Baruch slid the dough into the oven with the other loaves.

"Help, help, I want to come out!" the little dough cried.

The other loaves said: "Shh, little dough. We are hot, too, but we are patient. When we are ready, we will be delicious bread—and that's what is important."

At last, Baruch opened the oven door and took out all the loaves of bread. He took out the little challah loaf, too. It was warm and golden, and smelled yummy.

Baruch held up the little golden challah. He smiled a big smile. "How lovely you look! Now you are complete, and a perfect little challah!"

"Now I know why you poked and punched and pinched me," laughed the little challah. "I didn't like it, but now I am a beautiful challah, and that is what's important!"

Levi's father took him out of the tub and wrapped him in a big towel.

Levi cuddled up in the towel and turned to his father. "You know," he said. "I think I'm just like the little challah. It's hard for me just like it was hard for him. I don't like to get in the bath, but when it's over and I am nice and clean, I see that it was worth it."

"So you'll get right into the bath tomorrow night?" asked his father.

"Maybe," said Levi, smiling.